To Nianh,

I hope you enjoy

and all his adventures.

GW00788291

TAMBOW

With best wishes,

Charles Lamb

Raised in England miles from the sea, Charles Lamb was diagnosed at an early age to have salt-water instead of blood in his veins. Seizing every opportunity to get afloat, though not always staying afloat, he progressed from river-bound rafts to ocean sailing. After a few years in boat-building and yacht design, he moved to Greece to run charter yachts, then to the Caribbean. With family multiplying, it was back to England for a spell, and then he set sail with his wife, Caroline, and two small children back to the Caribbean and eventually settled in Canada. Tambow was born en route. After another sail down to South America and a few more Atlantic crossings, Charles and Caroline now spend much of their time on an ancient barge in SW France.

Charles Lamb

TAMBOW

Olympia Publishers
London

www.olympiapublishers.com
OLYMPIA PAPERBACK EDITION

Copyright © Charles Lamb 2010

The right of Charles Lamb to be identified as author of
this work has been asserted in accordance with sections 77 and 78 of the
Copyright, Designs and Patents Act 1988.

All Rights Reserved

No reproduction, copy or transmission of this publication
may be made without written permission.
No paragraph of this publication may be reproduced,
copied or transmitted save with the written permission of the publisher, or
in accordance with the provisions
of the Copyright Act 1956 (as amended).

Any person who commits any unauthorised act in relation to
this publication may be liable to criminal
prosecution and civil claims for damage.

A CIP catalogue record for this title is
available from the British Library.

ISBN: 978-1-84897-079-3

This is a work of fiction.
Names, characters, places and incidents originate from the writer's
imagination. Any resemblance to actual persons, living or dead, is purely
coincidental.

First Published in 2010

Olympia Publishers
60 Cannon Street
London
EC4N 6NP

Printed in Great Britain

To Zac & Zoe, who inspired me to write the stories.

Acknowledgments

Thanks to Caroline, my wife, for your faith in Tambow, and thanks to the many friends, young and old, who read the manuscripts, encouraged, edited, and generally helped the rascally little wombat to grow into a book.

CONTENTS

THE WOMBATS' ROUTE

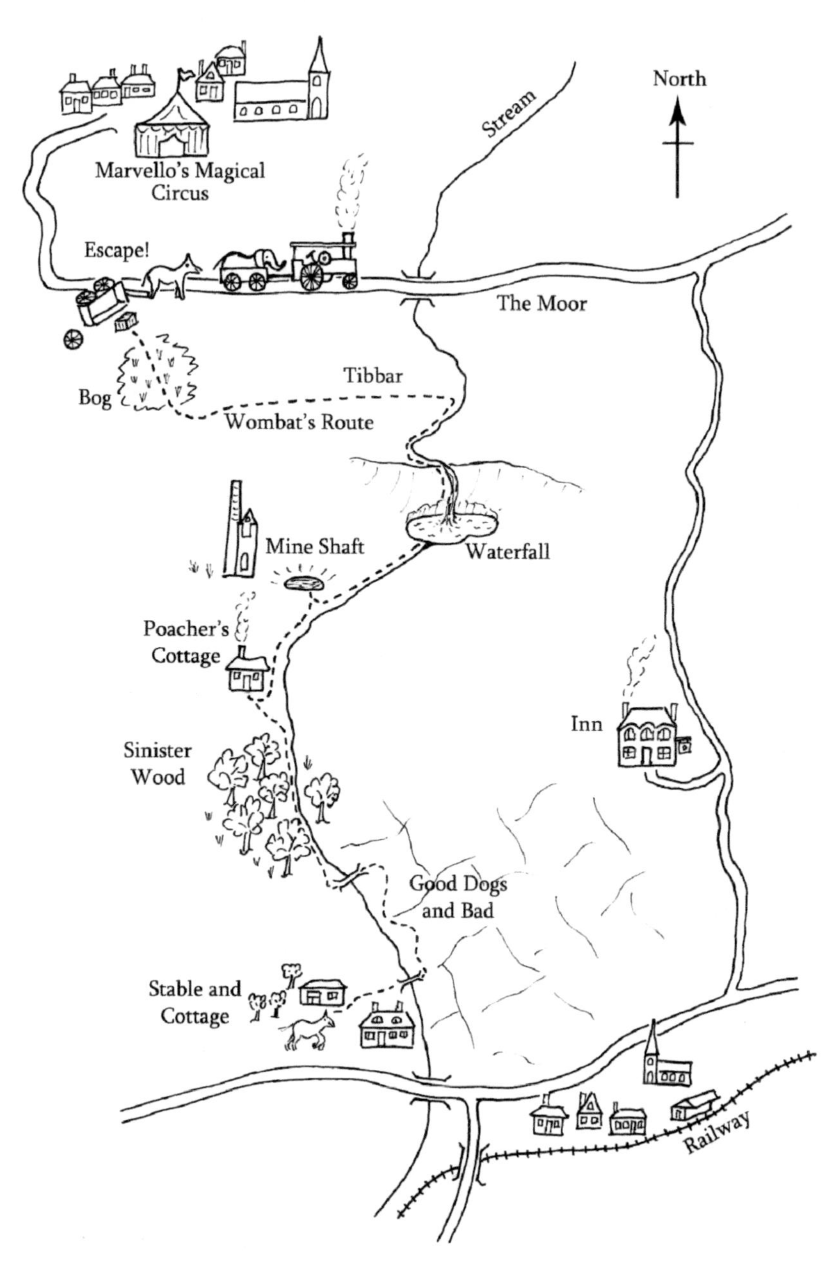

THIS WAY UP
WITH CARE

1. TAMBOW'S BIG BOUNCE

Tambow sat looking through the bars trying hard not to fidget, but young wombats find it difficult to sit still for long. When he thought his mother had fallen asleep, he tried an experimental somersault but got stuck upside down in the corner. After a bit of wriggling he untangled himself and practiced a few more rolls, crashing into the bars each time. Wombi sighed and burrowed deeper into the straw. She knew it was hopeless to try and quieten Tambow down when he was like this, so she put her paws over her eyes and pretended to be asleep.

The cage rocked alarmingly as Tambow bounced around inside. Bored with somersaults he tried jumping up and down to touch the roof of the cage and then had a go at headstands, but with the swaying of the wagon he kept falling over. He tried one more leap and as he took off, the wagon gave a great lurch as one of the wooden wheels dropped into a deep pothole. A loud splintering noise came from the wagon as the wheel spokes shattered and Tambow landed in a heap on his mother.

Wombi struggled out from beneath a tangle of straw, fur and paws. She was about to shout at Tambow when she suddenly realized the world was rushing past in a whirl. The overloaded wagon, its wheel broken, tipped over on its side, and as it crashed down onto the road, the jolt snapped the ropes holding their cage, allowing it to go rolling over and over until it came to a shuddering halt in the ditch beside the road.

Dazed, Wombi sat up and wondered what the squeaking noise was, while she waited for her head to stop spinning.

"Gerroff! Gerroff! I can't breathe and you're squashing me!"

She looked down, surprised to see she was now sitting on Tambow's head.

"Oh, I'm sorry dear, are you all right?" she

enquired anxiously as Tambow sat up and spat out a mouthful of straw.

"Wow! That was the best bounce I've ever done!" said Tambow.

"I don't think it was entirely your own doing, dear, I think something broke on the wagon and tipped us over," said his mother sensibly.

"Look, look, look!" shrieked Tambow excitedly, pointing to the end of the cage. "I broke the bars as well, wasn't that good, didn't I do well?" He wasn't going to be put off by explanations of broken wheels.

Sure enough, some of the bars at the end of the cage had bent and jumped out of place, leaving a gap just big enough for a wombat to get through. Beyond, the moor and freedom beckoned.

"Quick, Tambow, stop bouncing up and down! Keep quiet and follow me!" said Wombi, already squeezing through the bars. They cautiously climbed up the bank, out of the ditch and peered over the top. Men swarmed all around the upset wagon, some pushing and shoving, some yelling and waving their arms in the air and some releasing the poor horses from twisted shafts. They were all so busy that nobody noticed the missing cage.

Wombi put her paw to her lips, said, “Shh! Follow me,” and crept out of the ditch on the far side.

Keeping low she trotted swiftly away from the road and, glancing over her shoulder to make sure Tambow was following, picked her way through the prickly bushes, towards the open moor.

“Ouch!” The quiet was shattered by a cry from behind her. Tambow, who had been copying his mother by looking over his shoulder too, had walked straight into a large clump of brambles and was now backing out with his nose covered in prickles. He sat down with a thump on the ground and proceeded to pull out the prickles with his paws.

One of the crew of men now working on righting the wagon stopped pushing and said, “Ere, did you ’ear an owch?”

“Wot was that, Reg?” said Arthur, who had been driving the Big Top wagon.

“Oi ’eard an owch from over there,” said Reg, pointing to the moor across the ditch, as Wombi ran back to see what had happened to

Tambow.

"It's the wombats, they've escaped! Quick, after them!" yelled Arthur. They all left the stricken wagon and jumped across the ditch in pursuit, just as Wombi reached Tambow.

"Come on!" she cried. "They're after us, run!"

"But my dose hurts," he complained, holding a paw to it.

At that moment, Arthur let out a blood-curdling yell. When Tambow looked back to see what all the noise was about and saw all the angry men running towards him, he suddenly forgot about his nose and took off after his mother's bobbing tail.

That morning, as the sun rose over the edge of the moor, its first warm rays dispersed the lingering night mist and revealed a line of wagons jolting along the potholed road. The heavy horses strained at their shafts as they pulled the gaily painted carts along, their drivers occasionally cracking a whip above their heads and shouting encouragement whenever the wheels threatened to sink into the soft ruts. Leading the procession was a huge traction engine, its canopy festooned with brightly coloured lights and painted on either side with the words,

'MARVELLO'S MAGICAL CIRCUS'

Towed behind the engine, which hissed steam and belched out clouds of black smoke, came the biggest wagon of all.

Through the bars at the front of this big wagon, a large grey head sleepily peered out at the countryside as it slowly passed by. His huge ears flapped as smuts of soot floated down on him.

Tuskany the elephant was not in a good mood. He had enjoyed the town where the circus spent the last few days and had made friends with a small boy called Albert, the baker's son. Every morning, Albert had appeared with a bag full of stale buns and cakes left over from the previous day and smuggled them in to Tuskany when his keeper was not looking. Tuskany, of course, thoroughly enjoyed this treat and had been looking forward to it this morning, when he was rudely awakened and loaded into the wagon, no buns today!

Behind Tuskany came horse drawn carts carrying the lions and tigers, the dancing bear who was so clumsy and trod on everybody's toes, the chimpanzees who were always cheeky to the clowns, and all the other animals, large and small, who were kept busy in the circus.

The large wagon at the back of the line was laden with all the pieces of wood and canvas that went to make up the red and white striped Big Top, which the men put up every time they stopped at a town. Perched right on the top of this load was a small cage tied on with ropes and in the corner two small furry animals lay curled up on a bed of straw. A painted wooden board tied onto the side of the cage, announced, in rather shaky writing;

WOMBATS. HANDLE WITH CARE. THIS WAY UP.'

The smaller wombat opened one dark brown eye and looked at the landscape passing by. As far as the eye could see the moor rolled away, softly hued with greens and mauves and yellows in its summer colours. Trees were few and far between, with stunted, wind-contorted limbs, a reminder of the bleak winters they had to suffer.

He started to get up but a grey paw pressed him back into the straw. "Go back to sleep, Tambow, it's still early and I expect we've got a long way to go."

"I wish we could go and run about over there," he said, waving a paw in the direction of the moor. "It's so boring being cooped up in this little cage every day."

His mother, Wombi, opened her eyes and looked at him.

"So do I, dear, so do I. Before you were born, I used to live in a land similar to this, but it was much hotter. Then the trappers came and I've been stuck in cages ever since.

"It's not fair," said Tambow. "The only time they let us out is when they want us to do those silly tricks and then the trainer spends the whole time shouting at me because I'm no good at them."

Now Tambow had his wish. They raced

across the moor with the men in hot pursuit, dodging boulders and wriggling through bushes. Every time they thought they had lost them and ventured gingerly across open ground, a shout would go up from their pursuers and the chase would be on again.

To start with, Tambow thought this was a great game, but after a while his little legs started to feel tired and he was finding it difficult to keep up with Wombi. She kept urging him on and the shouts from behind kept his tired paws moving, but he desperately wanted a rest. How he wished he were small enough to be carried inside his mother's pouch, like he was when he was a baby.

Ahead, Wombi spotted an outcrop of large tumbled boulders, which looked like an ideal hiding place, but to get there they had to cross a wide flat area, dotted with small bright green grasses. She knew Tambow was tired and the men were catching up, but she urged him on and together they ran towards the cover.

As soon as they were out in the open they heard a triumphant yell from behind. "We've got 'em now lads, come on, after them!" The circus men, wearing their heavy boots, thundered across the springy turf behind the wombats, making the ground shake beneath their fleeing paws. They had covered half the distance to the rocks and the men were catching up fast when the wombats came upon a wet patch of grass where their paws sank in a little, slowing them down even more.

"I can't go any further," wailed Tambow between pants.

"You must," hissed Wombi. "Do you want to spend the rest of your life in a cage?" She glanced over her shoulder and thought it was hopeless. The men were nearly upon them but she stubbornly refused to give up.

Then a strange thing happened. Arthur, only a few paces behind them, his hands already outstretched, suddenly staggered as his boots sank through the bright green grass and into the soft bog beneath, then he tripped and fell flat on his face. The rest of the men tried to stop, but too late! They all found themselves sinking up to their knees in black, sticky mud, some joining Arthur, face first in the bog.

The wombats, being small and light, were able to keep going and a minute later they were safe in the shelter of the boulders looking back at the men floundering in the mire.

They both peeped out from behind a sun-warmed boulder, trying to regain their breath, and looked at the scene below. All the men had stumbled headlong into the bog guarding the rocky outcrop and now wallowed in the mud.

Eventually, the mucky circus crew removed themselves from the bog and scraped off the worst of the mud. The panting wombats, hidden from view, watched as the grimy men shook fists in their direction and then plodded off across the moor, retracing their steps towards the road.

2. A PLAN IS BORN

Tambow and Wombi watched the muddy circus men disappear into the distance and then roused themselves from their hiding place. They scrambled across the jumbled boulders and left their sanctuary, instinctively heading south, away from the road and the circus, guided by the mid-morning sun which hung lazily high in the sky, spreading its golden warmth across the silent moor.

They trotted along steadily with Wombi leading the way, picking her path around the dense patches of brambles, but always heading south. Tambow followed on behind, happy to be free to romp around in the sunshine now he had got his breath back after the frightening chase.

Wombi turned a corner in the path around a smooth, weather worn, granite boulder. Tambow following a few paces behind, was about to follow her when a movement on the rock caught his attention. He stopped and looked closer and saw a small creature sitting on the stone. It was green with a long tail, a tongue which flicked in and out and dark eyes which stared at him.

"Hello," said Tambow brightly. "Who are you?"

The lizard, the like of which Tambow had never seen before, stared back, motionless except for his little black eyes which blinked rapidly. Then the tiny tongue flickered out and Tambow waited breathlessly for a reply.

When he didn't receive one, he said, "I'm Tambow and I am a Wombat!"

He moved in for a closer look and pressed his face up against the rock, just below the blinking eyes. The lizard, alarmed by this latest move, scuttled off backwards and disappeared into a small cleft where he bravely flicked his tongue out again. Tambow scampered across the rock and pressed his nose into the crack.

"Don't run away, I only thought you might like to play."

Meanwhile, Wombi eventually noticed the absence of her son and returned to find him. She rounded the boulder and saw him perched on the top of it, with his nose seemingly buried in it.

"Tambow! What are you doing? Stop talking to that rock and come down here at once!" she shouted up at him.

Startled, Tambow jumped in the air but only his tail and back paws moved.

"I'm duck!"

"You're what?"

"I'd god my dose duck in dis crack. 'Elp, ged me out!" Tambow cried, beginning to panic.

Wombi sighed and climbed up the rock after him. She took a firm hold of his tail with her front paws, braced her back paws against the stone and pulled hard.

"Ouch!" cried Tambow, "Oh my dail! Oh my dose!"

He finally came out with a pop. Wombi fell over backwards and rolled off the rock and Tambow landed in a heap on top of her.

Wombi pushed Tambow off her and said, "Do try to keep up dear, we've got a long way to go and we will never get there if you keep dawdling."

"Well, where are we going and when is lunch?" Tambow asked feeling suddenly hungry.

"I don't know about lunch, we'll have to see what we can find, but I'll tell you where we are going as we walk along," Wombi replied. "Your father and I used to live in a land across the sea, where it was always warm and we had lots of friends and relations. I've never seen any other wombats in this land so we must try and get home. When we were captured, we were put in a ship and we sailed across the sea for many moons. I think we will have to get back to the sea and find a ship to take us home."

Tambow didn't understand much of what his mother said, but the mention of his father did trigger off a question.

"Will father ever be coming back to us?"

Wombi looked down sadly at her son trotting by her side. "I don't think so dear. He's gone to join the other wombats in the sky and I don't think he'll ever come down."

Tambow had never been quite sure where his father, Wambot, had gone, but he remembered he had loved him very much and missed him when he disappeared. Unfortunately, Wambot had been rather rash and one day, when the Daring D'Arcy of the Human Cannon caught a cold and couldn't perform, Wambot offered to take his place. Sadly, no one thought to put less gunpowder in the cannon and Wambot had been much lighter than D'Arcy. When the smoke cleared there had been no sign of Wambot except for a ragged hole in the roof of the Big Top. He had never been seen again and the ringmaster said perhaps he'd gone into orbit. Tambow missed his father and was inclined to cry when he saw a shooting star.

They trotted along for a little longer and then they came to a small stream. Its clear waters chuckled and gurgled around rocks and little islands of moss as it busily flowed down the gentle slope. The wombats stopped for a long drink of the cool refreshing water and then sat beside the stream for a rest.

Wombi looked at it thoughtfully for a while and then said to Tambow, “I think if we follow the stream, it will lead us eventually down to the sea. Yes, that’s what we’ll do. Come on!”

Tambow, who was looking forward to a snooze in the sun, got back on his paws, sighed, and chased after his mother who was already trotting down the hill beside the stream.

“I’m beginning to wonder if bouncing the cage off the wagon was such a good idea after all,” he grumbled to himself as his tummy rumbled, reminding him that now was about the time the circus usually stopped for lunch.

All afternoon they walked along and could only find a few berries to eat. Everything on the moor seemed to be prickly or tough and not to a young wombat’s taste at all.

As the sun was setting they found a large overhanging boulder of granite, which formed a natural cave, and decided to settle there for the night.

Wombi sent Tambow off to find some dry bracken for their bed and then went to look for something to eat. Not too far away, she found a bush with a good crop of berries and she picked the ripest of these. Eating a few herself she carried the rest back to the cave expecting to see Tambow and a pile of bracken. There was no sign of either. Worried, she put the berries down and went off in search of him. She hadn't gone far when she noticed a small tree on the far side of the stream, acting in a very strange fashion. Instead of standing up straight as trees usually do, it thrashed about, and every now and then it stopped and sounded like it was licking its lips.

She stood across the stream from the tree and soon saw the reason. "Tambow, what are you doing up there?"

"Oh, hello. Berries, lots of yummy berries," he said, reaching out to grab a particularly succulent pawful of elderberries at the end of a branch. It was just out of reach and he wriggled a bit further along the branch when CRRAAAK, the branch broke and Tambow came tumbling out of the tree to land with a splash in the middle of the shallow stream. Wombi waded in and pulled him onto his paws by the scruff of his neck.

“Now you are in,” she said, “you might as well have a good wash.”

He wriggled to get free because he really did not like washing, but his mother held him firmly until she was satisfied he was clean from his nose to the tip of his tail. Tambow scrambled to the bank, climbed out and had a good shake. He couldn’t understand this obsession grown-ups had about washing!

They collected some bracken together and by the time they’d made a comfortable bed for themselves, Tambow had dried off and the sun was setting on the horizon. They sat in the entrance to the cave watching the red glow filling the sky as the sun disappeared from view.

It was quite dark at the back of the cave when they settled down on their bed. Tambow snuggled up close to Wombi and she put a reassuring paw around him as they lay there quietly, listening to the faint gurgling of the stream. No other sound disturbed their peaceful world and when she heard a gentle snoring coming from Tambow, she smiled and was soon asleep herself.

3. THE FOX MISSES BREAKFAST

THUMP, THUMP, THUMP.

Wombi stirred in her sleep and was then instantly awake as the thumping noise came again.

THUMP, THUMP, THUMP.

“Tambow, wake up!” she hissed quietly to the gently snoring wombat.

Tambow stirred and sleepily opened one eye, which slowly focused on his mother.

“Wassamatter? Is it breakfast time already?”

“Shhh, and lie still, I heard a strange noise and I don’t know what it was,” she said, putting a paw on his shoulder to prevent him from sitting up.

A grey shape passed the cave entrance, followed by another and then another.

Close behind the third there followed a much larger shape running hard. It had a long bushy tail, held straight out behind. Tambow wriggled around so that Wombi was between him and the cave entrance and then peered past her to watch and see what happened next.

He heard the faint pounding of paws on the soft springy turf and then one small shape, followed closely by the large one, tore past the cave in a blur. Tambow sat wondering if this was a game of early morning tag and if anyone could join in, when there was a sudden flurry of skidding paws in the entrance. The smaller shape came bounding straight at them, swerved in fright at the last moment when it spotted the wombats, bounced off the wall and came to a halt upside down at the back of the cave.

"I say," said Tambow, "can anyone join in?"

"Shhh, Tambow, keep behind me!" Wombi said urgently as she heard stealthy noises at the cave entrance.

Tambow stared at the newcomer, who by this time had righted himself and sat in the corner trembling, whiskers quivering and eyes bulging with fright.

"Who are you?" whispered Tambow. He had never seen a rabbit before and was a bit puzzled by his dramatic arrival.

"I'm Tibbar, I'm a rabbit," squeaked the terrified animal. "Wh-who are you?" He'd never seen an animal like this one on the moor and didn't know if it was fierce or not.

"I know you are a rabbit," came a deep voice from outside the cave. "Why don't you come out so we can finish our little game, or do you want me to come in and find you?"

"Oh!" squeaked Tibbar, burying his nose in the bracken bed and putting his paws over his long ears.

"I'm coming!" and a long thin nose appeared in the entrance, followed by two bright, shifty eyes and a pair of ears, which stood smartly to attention.

Wombi leapt to her paws and hissed, "Get out, go away and leave us alone." Her fur bristled and she seemed to grow to twice her

size.

The fox, expecting to find a small, solitary rabbit, jumped back in surprise and banged his head on the roof of the small cave. He backed off and sat down outside the entrance. Staring hard into the gloomy interior, he saw the dark round shape of a strange animal and another pair of eyes peeping brightly from behind. Right at the back of the cave, he spied the small white blur of the rabbit's tail.

"Good morning," the fox said, trying hard now to be polite and ignore his aching head. "I didn't know anybody lived here. I wonder if you would be kind enough to send that young rabbit out to me, he's, er, he's late for school."

A shrill squeak came from the back of the cave, as the rabbit tried to disappear into the bracken.

"Late for your breakfast you mean," said Wombi.

But the fox was persistent. "Well, if you would like to share my breakfast, no doubt we could come to some arrangement, but it is only a small rabbit. I'll tell you what, let me have that little chap and I'll go and find you a nice fat rabbit," he lied.

"Well, I'll tell you what. You are not having it, so you'd better go and find your breakfast elsewhere!" said Wombi bravely, crossing her toes and hoping the fox would go, as she was becoming frightened by his menacing face and scary teeth.

"Now look here, you overgrown rodent," said the fox, losing his temper, "I don't know what you are but if you think you can arrive here and start ordering me about, you've got another thing coming."

"We are wombats and where we come from we eat bigger animals than you," Wombi bluffed. "Now go away before you make me angry."

"Oh," said the fox, "no offence meant, just passing and thought I'd pop in and say hello. Well must be off, can't stay here chattering, things to do." He backed away as he spoke and then abruptly turned tail and rushed off.

Wombi breathed a sigh of relief and turned round to Tambow and the rabbit. Tambow looked at his mother with sudden respect at this show of bravery, wondering how a wombat could eat such a fierce looking animal. The rabbit pulled his head out of the bracken and fixed his great big eyes on Wombi.

"D-dddddo you really eat f-foxes?," he asked nervously, thinking he might be regarded as a mere snack by this strange animal.

"Do we eat foxes?" butted in Tambow. "I should say we do, and lions and tigers and elephants and circus trainers and..."

"Don't be silly, dear, you know we don't. I said that to get him to go away.

Now," she said, turning to the rabbit, "did you say your name was Tibbar?"

"Ye-yes. You're not going to eat me are you?" he inquired nervously.

"Goodness me, no! My name is Wombi and this is Tambow. We are wombats and are following this stream until we find the sea."

"What's a sea?" asked Tibbar.

"It's a, well it's sort of, oh, never mind. Where's the rest of your family? They must be getting worried about you," said Wombi, noticing for the first time that Tibbar was a very young animal.

"I expect they are all hiding in the burrow.

Would you mind looking outside to see if the fox has really gone? I ought to be getting home," replied Tibbar.

"Show us the way and we'll come with you, just to be sure," said Wombi.

"Oh thank you, it's not far," said the grateful little rabbit.

The three animals emerged from the cave as the first rays of the sun crept over the hill behind them, sweeping away any dark corners where the fox may have hidden. Reassured, they trotted across the moor until they came to some grassy humps, which were riddled with holes. It seemed deserted as Tibbar led them to one hole and said, "This is where I live."

Wombi went to the entrance and called out, "Hulloooooo, is anybody at hoooome?"

A moment later a face appeared cautiously at the entrance. "Um, yes, me. Can I help?"

"We've brought Tibbar back."

"TIBBAR!" the rabbit yelled as she bounded out of the burrow. "Oh, Tibbar, we thought the fox had eaten you!"

Rabbits started popping out of the burrows all around them and dancing about with excitement when they saw Tibbar, safely home again. Tambow, never one to miss out on a bit of fun, started jumping about too, until he tripped over backwards and sat on Tibbar's grandfather, who took exception to this rough treatment and bit him.

"Ouch!" cried Tambow, hopping about on three paws as he tried to feel what damage had been done to the fourth.

"Serves you right," said Wombi. "I'm always telling you to look before you bounce. Come on, we must leave these rabbits to their reunion."

"Oh no!" chorused the rabbits, "you must stay and have something to eat with us, you can't go yet."

"Well..." said Wombi.

"Oh, yes please," said Tambow, suddenly feeling hungry at the mention of food.

"Good, that's settled then," said Tibbar's mother.

A number of rabbits rushed off to their holes and moments later reappeared, dragging behind them carrots, lettuce leaves and other succulent titbits, which they piled up in front of the wombats.

"No berries?" asked Tambow hopefully, and winced as his mother cuffed him around the ear.

They tucked in to breakfast and as they ate, Wombi asked some of the older rabbits about the stream and where it led. Unfortunately, they were a rather unadventurous lot and never strayed far from their burrows, so they were unable to help. When the wombats had eaten their fill and were ready to leave, they did insist that Wombi filled her pouch with as much food as she could carry.

Tambow asked if he might stay and play with Tibbar, but Wombi put her paw down and said they must be on their way. The rabbits were secretly relieved as they were a bit alarmed by the large bouncy wombat, and none of them really relished the thought of being sat on like Tibbar's grandfather.

They made their farewells and both received a big thank you from Tibbar and his parents, then set off down the stream once more, following the sparkling clear water to wherever it might lead.

4. THE DARK PIT

Refreshed by a good night's sleep and a fine breakfast, the two wombats trotted down the valley, enjoying the hot sun on their backs. The moorland rolled in gentle slopes about them whilst the stream meandered along, slowing and widening into shallow pools, bordered by bright green bog grasses, and then racing down a little valley, cutting a narrow channel as the water tumbled around rocks and over roots.

A butterfly rose from the grass beneath Tambow's paws and fluttered across the heather. He raced after it, jumping up onto his hind legs and trying to catch it with his fore paws, but each time it moved tantalizingly out of reach. Wombi patiently waited for him to wear himself out and it wasn't long before he tripped over a root and went sprawling in the heather, allowing the butterfly to continue on its leisurely way. Tambow sheepishly trotted back to his mother and together they continued their journey.

A while later, progress by the stream became more difficult as it entered a steep sided valley, with scrub and gorse growing right to the edge in places.

They crossed the stream by hopping over some tumbled rocks, which lay conveniently like stepping-stones. On the far bank they found a path, not very wide but well trodden. Following the path, the valley became steeper and steeper, with the water rushing over the stones, sparkling in the sunlight.

Wombi stopped suddenly and was nearly bowled over by Tambow as he walked into her, tripped and fell into a bush, interested in everything as usual except where he was going. She helped him up and then held up a paw to silence the flood of questions, which always seemed to be on the tip of his tongue.

"Listen," she said, frowning. "Can you

hear anything?"

Tambow cocked his head on one side, put a thoughtful, listening look on his face and then said, "No."

Wombi shook her head, sighing, and made a mental note to wash out his ears next time she got him in the water. She led the way on down the path, stopping again a little while later.

"You must be able to hear something now," she said.

Tambow put his listening look on again and then said, "I can hear my tummy rumbling, is that what you mean?"

"No! I can hear a thundery sort of noise and it seems to be getting louder," she explained patiently.

He looked up at the clear blue sky with a thoughtful expression and, after a few moments, suggested it might be about to rain if there was thunder about. Wombi gave him a withering look and carried on beside the stream.

Soon, the thundery sort of noise became so loud that even Tambow could hear it. They rounded a bend in the narrow valley and then stopped abruptly as they found themselves at the top of a high waterfall. The stream seemed to shoot out into space and then it shimmered as it dropped through the bright sunlight, finally plunging into a shady pool a long way below.

The wombats peered over the drop and saw the path continue down the side of the fall, scrambling from rock to rock, following narrow ledges and negotiating steep slopes until it finally rejoined the stream a long way below.

"Now follow me and be careful," warned his mother. "It's very steep down there, so don't slip and NO bouncing!"

Tambow gave her a look as if to say, 'What! Me bounce?' and then followed her over the edge.

They climbed down the steep path, carefully creeping along the narrow sections and trying hard not to look down, jumping some of the easier rocks and slithering where the loose stones lay on the slope. Half-way down, the going became easier and so Wombi stopped worrying about Tambow and carried on to the bottom. Meanwhile, Tambow decided to have a closer look at the waterfall.

He hopped across the boulders, getting nearer and nearer to the tumbling water. The rocks near the fall were slippery with centuries of spray and mossy growth. He stood precariously on a rounded stone near the cascade and admired a little rainbow, which seemed to spring from the fall itself and arch out into the bright sunshine. The colours shimmered as the spray drifted in the gentle breeze and Tambow put out a paw to see what a rainbow felt like. It moved tantalizingly as he reached out and so he leant forward a little further.

Whoops! His paws slipped on the wet moss and he found himself falling out into space. “Heeeeeeelp!” he cried as he tumbled over and over, until, with a big splash he landed in the water below. He arrived with a BUMP at the bottom of the pool, his eyes screwed tightly shut and holding his breath.

Wondering which way was up, he experimentally opened his eyes and was relieved to find his head didn’t fill up with

water. A fish swam into view and stopped to look at him, both surprised to see each other there. Tambow started to say 'hello', but it came out as more of a gurgle and frightened the fish away. He was beginning to think talking underwater was not the right thing to do, as he was finding breathing a bit puzzling, when something grabbed him by the scruff of the neck and hauled him to the surface.

Coughing and spluttering, Tambow splashed his paws about as Wombi pulled him to the bank of the pool. She hauled him up the grassy slope and dumped the soggy animal in a heap. He looked about feebly, for once speechless, as the water ran out of his fur.

"Tambow, when will you ever learn to look where you're going?" Wombi was furious as she didn't like swimming and hadn't enjoyed her dip to rescue him.

"But I was looking all the time. Except my paws. I think they might have been looking the wrong way," he admitted. "Sorry."

They climbed up the slope away from the pool, until they were back in the sunshine, and then had a good roll in the warm grass, ending up with a vigorous shake, which sent a shower of droplets and grass seeds over an unsuspecting frog. Wombi politely apologized, but the frog, being unused to strangers, hopped off down the slope and disappeared into the pool with a splash.

Steaming gently in the warm sun, the wombats continued their journey along the path, which now wound between thickets of gorse and bracken a little distance from the stream. The valley twisted to and fro, the path with it, and Tambow trotted along in his mother's wake, trying to keep in her paw prints. As his legs were shorter, he found he had to keep taking an extra half step to catch up, but then, he could never remember whether to lead off with his left paw or his right, and so he was continuously in a muddle.

Coming around one bend, Wombi suddenly squeaked and jumped into the bracken at the side of the path, hissing over her shoulder, "Quick, follow me!" Tambow looked up and followed, noticing, before he nosed into the undergrowth, a small cottage further down the path and striding up the path towards them, a man with a scruffy beard and a face like thunder.

Tambow wriggled through the thick tangle, following Wombi's trail, when he heard a loud squeak from in front, followed by a long gasp and then a dull thud.

"Wombi, are you all right?"

"I've fallen down a hole," came the faint reply. "Don't come any closer!"

"When will you ever learn to look where you're going?" mimicked Tambow, settling down beneath a gorse bush.

"This is no time for jokes! I'm stuck and we mustn't let that man find us!"

"How far down are you?" asked Tambow.

"Not far, I'm on a sort of ledge. I think the bottom of the hole is much further down but I can't see it. Keep quiet and out of sight until the man has gone, and we'll think of something."

Tambow heard the crunch of heavy boots on the path and breathed a sigh of relief as they passed his hiding place. He listened as they started to fade into the distance and then his heart stopped as he heard them coming back again. Slow, uncertain footsteps shuffled around for a while and then he heard the bushes being pushed to one side as the man followed the wombats' trail. Tambow crawled deeper into the undergrowth as silently as he could.

The man was a poacher and whilst walking up the path on his way to check his traps, he suddenly became aware of some strange animal tracks, the like of which he had never seen before. They seemed to be going down the path, so he turned and followed them. He scratched his head but couldn't make it out, the animal seemed to have a varying amount of legs between four and eight. He scratched his head again and thought about it, eventually deciding it must be an eight-legged animal, which was lame in four legs and only used them occasionally. He tugged at his beard and tried to remember if he had ever seen an eight-legged animal before and decided he hadn't, so he thought he would follow the trail to see where it led.

Returning down the hill, the poacher could see where the strange animal had left the path from the flattened grass at the side, so he pushed through the undergrowth and followed the tracks. Unbeknown to him, his boots passed within a whisker of Tambow, hiding under a gorse bush with his paws pressed tightly over his head, hoping he resembled a blade of grass. A few feet further on, the man stopped suddenly as a gaping black hole appeared in front of him.

"Well Oi'll be blowed, twenty-five years Oi've lived 'ere and Oi never knewed that was there. 'Course," the poacher continued to himself, "there be lots of old mines about these 'ere parts." With that, he picked up a handful of small stones and tossed them down the hole.

"Ouch!" The single word floated up out of the ground, followed by its echo and then the noise of some of the stones landing at the bottom, a long way down.

"Who be down there?" asked the poacher in surprise.

"Me," came the timid reply.

"Oh!" said the poacher, absorbing this information. "Who be me?"

"I am," said Wombi, unhelpfully.

"Arhh, but what are you, and what are you

doing down this 'ere 'ole?" he said, determined to get to the bottom of it, the mystery that is, not the hole.

"I'm a wombat and I fell down the hole. Will you help me get out please?" she asked politely.

"Wombat eh! Now where 'ave Oi 'eard about wombats?" He tugged at his beard and thought deeply. "Oi remember now, met a fellow from a circus t'other day when I went to the market. Said he'd lost a pair of wombats and was putting out a reward for them, Oi could do with that money, where's the other one?"

"Err, he fell down another hole, miles away," Wombi quickly replied.

"Oh well, 'alf a reward is better than no reward Oi suppose." He had a sudden thought. "Ere, 'ow many legs 'ave you got?"

Wombi, who couldn't count, thought for a moment and then replied, "Lots."

"That's all right then, don't go away. Oi'll be back directly with a rope and get you out." With that he stomped off back to the path and headed down the hill towards his cottage.

Thoughts of the reward made him whistle cheerily as he strode along.

As the footsteps faded, Tambow crawled out from his hiding place and cautiously approached the edge of the mine shaft. He peered down into the inky darkness, but could see nothing. As he stood on the edge the loose ground slipped beneath his paws and he stepped back in alarm as earth and stones clattered down the hole.

"Tambow, is that you?"

"Yes, what are we going to do?" asked the frightened little wombat.

"You must keep out of sight of the man. Whatever you do, don't let him know you are around. When he gets me out of here, I'll try and escape and join you further down the stream. Go now, keep well away from the house and wait for me."

"But..." began Tambow.

"No buts," said Wombi urgently, "you must go now before he comes back. Go on, I'll be all right and I'll catch up with you soon. Take care!"

"You too. Bye bye, Wombi," he said, with

a quiver in his voice. He backed away from the hole and carefully made his way up the hillside, pushing through the tangled brambles until he climbed up, out of the valley, and came to the open slopes above. He trotted on until the path was a distant dark line on the valley floor and then, feeling safe from the strange man with the beard, he stopped for a rest.

After a while, Tambow saw a tiny figure emerge from the far off cottage and he watched as it walked up the valley path. Soon, he was able to make out something slung over the man's shoulder, but he was too far away to see what it was so, fearing the worst for his mother's safety, Tambow decided to stay and watch.

5. TAMBOW TO THE RESCUE

Wombi waited nervously on the narrow ledge, keeping away from the edge as the mineshaft seemed to disappear forever below her. High above, she could see the clouds floating past a circle of blue sky, but even her long claws couldn't help her climb the smooth side.

She worried about Tambow, sure that he wouldn't be able to keep out of trouble without her there to guide him. Suddenly, all thoughts of Tambow disappeared when a coil of rope bounced on the ledge, nearly knocking her off and making her jump with fright. The end of the rope slithered down and disappeared into the inky blackness. Looking up, she could see it leading over the rim of the shaft.

As she looked, a pair of boots appeared, outlined against the sky and then the rest of the man followed, sliding down the rope. A yellow glow from a candle lamp tied to his belt faintly illuminated the shaft as he descended to where Wombi was huddled. His feet thumped on the rock and then he stood there, peering at Wombi, whilst his eyes became accustomed to the dim light.

"Why, you've only got four legs!" he said, surprised.

Wombi, not knowing how many four was, looked down, suddenly alarmed and thinking perhaps she had lost one in the fall. She was relieved to see she had the same number of legs as usual, but couldn't understand his strange remark at all.

Looking at him suspiciously she asked, "Have you come to get me out of this hole or are you just here to make silly remarks?"

"Oh, Oi've come to get you out, don't worry. Valuable little animal you are. Now get into this and Oi'll have you out in no time." He held open a sack, which had been tucked inside his shirt, and moved towards Wombi.

Wombi, now thoroughly alarmed by this strange man, had no intention of letting herself be trapped in a sack. She backed away from him, but soon felt one of her back paws slip over the edge and she could retreat no further.

"Come on my beauty, there's nothing to be afraid of!" His big hand shot out and before Wombi could do anything, the poacher grabbed her by the scruff of the neck and she was dangling helplessly from his arm.

"You great bully, put me down," she squealed as she wriggled helplessly.

With his free hand, he opened the sack and dropped the struggling wombat inside, and then he tied the top with a piece of rope and dumped the bundle on the ledge. Ignoring the muffled protests, the poacher hauled up the end of rope and tied it securely to the wriggling sack. Then, with much puffing and grunting, he climbed up the rope and out of the mineshaft.

Back in the sunlight, he blew out his candle lamp and started to pull up the rope. Wombi dangled from the end like a sack of potatoes and every time it bumped into the side

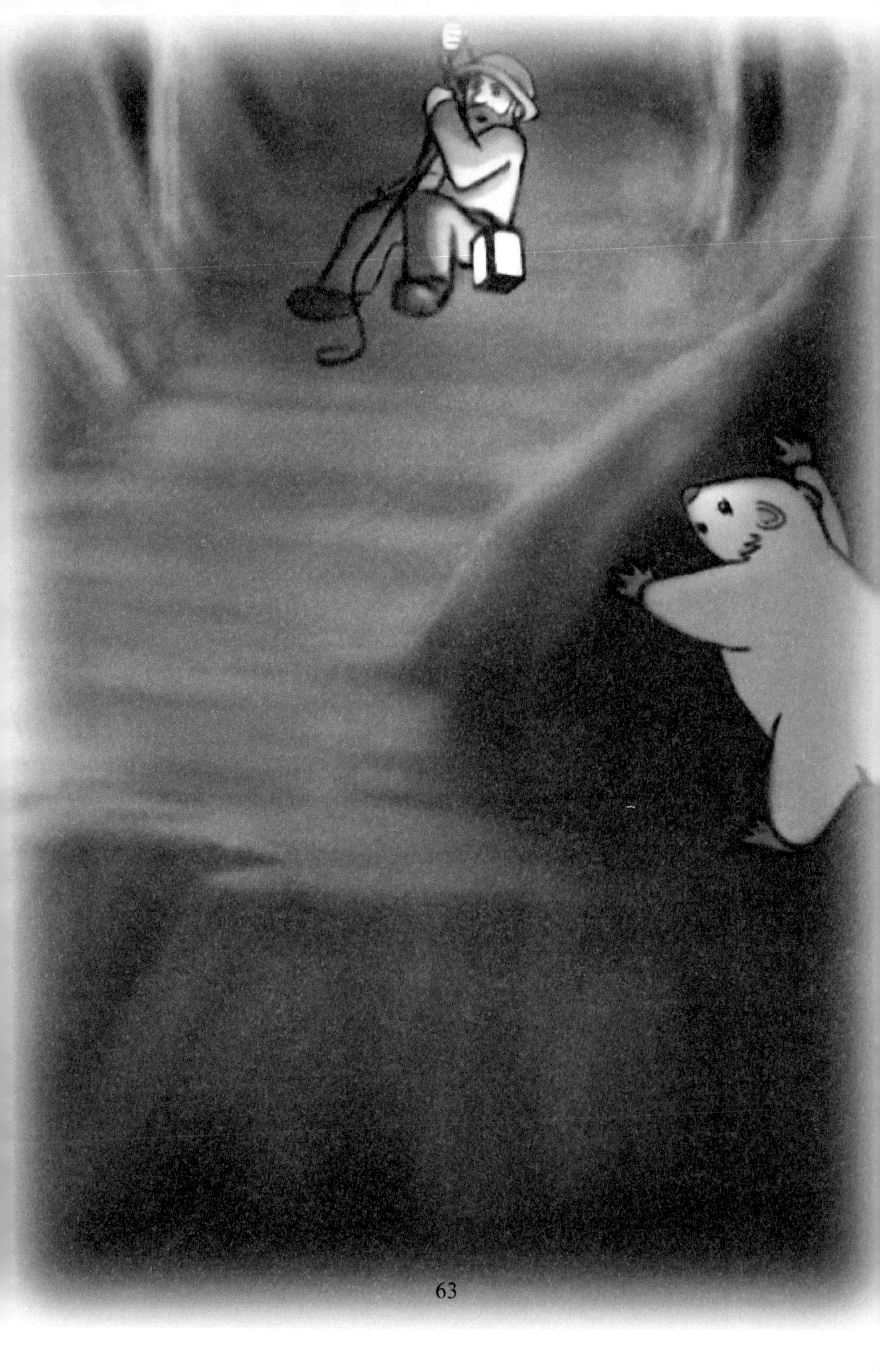

of the shaft she squeaked with fright and surprise. A last bump and she was out of the mineshaft, then the poacher left her in an untidy heap on the grass while he untied the rope from a tree and coiled it up. Slinging the rope across one shoulder, he picked up the sack with Wombi still in it and set off, back to the path.

As he walked along with Wombi swinging by his side, the poacher whistled happily as he thought about the five gold coins, offered as a reward for the capture of the wombats.

He strode down the valley and soon came to his little cottage. Rough stone walls supported a sagging roof, tiled with slates, some of which had slipped, and a few of which were missing altogether. At the front of the cottage, paint peeled from two small windows with wooden shutters, a solid looking door stood between them. Smoke spiralled lazily up into the still air from a crooked chimney built precariously on one end wall.

A few chickens scratched in the dirt outside the cottage, hopefully looking for a morsel which may have been overlooked in the previous day's search. They clucked furiously, their heads bobbing to and fro as they ran from beneath the poacher's feet, and then stood in a huddle, heads down, tails up, as they gossiped away.

"Whaaat d'you think is in that sack? Cluck, cluck."

"Ahiiii don't know, been poaching again I expect. Cluck."

"Perhaps he's caught the fox. Cluck, cluck."

"Cluck, cluck, cluuuuuck!"

The door squeaked as it was pushed open, the hinges long overdue for some oil. Inside, the smoke laden air was quite gloomy until the poacher threw open one of the shuttered windows. A battered table and two chairs stood in front of the soot blackened cooking stove and at the far end of the single room, a straw stuffed mattress served as his bed. In one corner stood two chicken coops made of woven hazel, which he sometimes used to take chickens to market.

Dumping Wombi, still in the sack, upon the table, he went and fetched one of the coops.

Opening the little door and untying the neck of the sack, he carefully tipped Wombi into the coop and then shut the door on her, fixing it securely with a twist of wire.

Wombi glared at him from behind the bars. "Let me out, I haven't done you any harm. You can't keep me shut up in this horrid little cage."

"It won't be for long, my beauty. Tonight Oi'll take you along to the inn where your owner will no doubt reward me for your return." He then rummaged about near the stove, pulled out a large flagon and poured himself a mug of ale. Opening a box, he found a crust of stale looking bread and a piece of hard cheese. After wolfing down his meagre lunch, he closed the shutter on the window, checked the cage was secure, and then pulled the door shut as he went out, the latch clicking securely into place.

Left on the table in the half-light, Wombi inspected the cage to see if there was any way out. The sticks were woven too closely together to be able to get her teeth around one to try chewing her way out and the wire holding the door shut was firmly twisted on the outside, out of reach of her paws.

"Oh, bother!" she sighed. Things really did seem hopeless. She started to think about Tambow and that worried her even more. The poor little chap would be waiting all alone for her and wouldn't know what to do when she didn't turn up. She tried hard not to cry but couldn't prevent a tear from rolling down her cheek. She wiped it with the back of a furry paw but others followed it and soon she was sobbing uncontrollably into both paws.

From his hiding place up the hill, Tambow watched as the poacher returned to his cottage. The worried little wombat scratched his head and wondered what to do next, then he decided to watch and wait until the man left, and then see what could be done. He settled down on the warm grass, hidden by some boulders, and fixed his beady eyes on the doorway, determined not to let it out of his sight for an instant.

Sometime later, he awoke with a start when he heard a noise. He sat up hurriedly, wondering where he was until he spotted the poacher shutting the door and taking the path back up the valley. He waited breathlessly until the man was out of sight and then left his cover and hurried down the hillside towards the cottage.

He crept silently up towards the door and was nearly there when a noise beside him made him jump with fright.

"Whaaaat do you want? Cluck, cluck."

Tambow spun around to see a large, angry looking chicken standing behind him. He backed away a few paces but the chicken followed him, it's red crested head dancing around. Tambow's tail bumped into the door and he could retreat no further, so he stood and stared at the chicken, which stared back.

"Arrrrrrrre you deaf? Cluck, cluck. I said whaaaaat do you want? Cluck."

"No. I am not deaf," said Tambow indignantly. "I've come to find my mother."

"Oh, oh, oh, oh, cluck, cluck. What does she look like? Cluck."

"Like me," said Tambow, "but bigger."

"Not seen her then, cluck. Oh, waaaaait a minute, would she have been wearing a sack?

Cluck, cluck."

"Yes, that's right," his ears pricked up excitedly, "that man brought her here in a sack."

"Oh well, oh well, don't know where she is then. Might be inside, might be inside. Cluck."

"Wombi! Wombi!" he called out.

"Tambow? Oh, Tambow, is that really you?" a faint reply came back.

"Don't worry Wombi, I'll get you out," he said with confidence, and then wondered how he was going to manage it. The door looked awfully solid and the latch was a long way out of his reach. He walked all the way around the cottage, but there were no other doors or windows apart from those at the front.

He inspected the windows carefully, but they were both firmly shuttered. He tried to reach the latch on the door, but even his highest jump was a long way short of it. He walked around to the back again and noticed that a thick stem of ivy grew up to the eaves. With the vague idea that he might be able to reach the latch if he dropped down from above, he started to climb. When he got to the top and scrambled onto the roof, he looked down and instantly wished he hadn't. He wasn't used to heights and his tummy suddenly felt quite funny.

He forced himself to look up again and started to climb towards the ridge. His paws slid on the weather worn slates and he was relieved when he got to the top and could rest on the ridge of the roof. Hoping he could crawl down the other side to get above the doorway, and perhaps be able to drop down and grab the latch, he set off backwards down the roof but found himself sliding down the smooth tiles faster and faster, unable to stop.

His paws scrabbled frantically, trying to find a secure hold, and then they chanced on a patch of loose tiles which flew out from beneath his claws. Tiles showered down, shattering on the hard ground below, and Tambow found he had exposed a large hole in the roof. He promptly fell through the hole and disappeared into the dark interior.

With his eyes tightly closed, poor Tambow barely had a moment to think, "Oh! Help!" as he tumbled down, when his descent was interrupted by something uncomfortable which squeaked. Opening his eyes, he saw he had crash-landed on Wombi's cage, bursting it open and allowing his mother to crawl out unharmed from the wreckage. Overjoyed, Tambow jumped off the remains of the cage and gave Wombi a crushing hug.

"Oh, Tambow! I'm so pleased to see you," said Wombi when she finally managed to wriggle out of his embrace. "How did you know I was stuck, I thought you would have been waiting down the valley?"

"I watched from the hill," Tambow proudly replied. "When I saw the man leave without you, I came down and looked around for a way in." He looked up at the hole in the roof, high above, and an uneasy thought struck him. "Er, how do we get out again?"

"Under the door," said Wombi, positively.

Tambow looked at the narrow crack of light shining under the door. Breakfast seemed like a distant memory, but on inspecting his tummy it appeared just as large as normal. There was no way it would squeeze through that tiny gap.

Whilst he puzzled over the problem, Wombi hopped off the table and went over to the door. With her tail up and nose down, she tore into the hard earthen floor with her front paws. Her long claws furrowed the earth deeply and sent showers of soil shooting out behind her. Tambow, who followed to see what she had in mind, got the first lot full in the face and he had to step smartly to one side to avoid the rest.

Spitting the dry earth from his mouth, Tambow asked, "What are you doing?"

"Digging a tunnel under the door," said Wombi as she stopped for a rest. "I forgot you always lived in a cage so you haven't learnt about tunnelling yet. Just you watch, this is what wombats are best at!"

Without any further ado, she began her busy excavating again. Soon, she was half-way under the door and a few moments later she disappeared completely. She was free!

"Come on, Tambow," she called from outside, "the man might come back any minute. We must hurry!"

Without needing any further encouragement, Tambow wriggled through the hole and out into the sunshine again. The two wombats raced side by side across the yard towards the open country beyond, scattering alarmed and noisy chickens as they went.

Hearing the din from the chickens as he returned from checking his traps on the moor, the poacher hurried around the last bend in the path, just in time to see the fleeting grey shapes of the wombats tearing off down the valley.

"Oi! You come back here, you little varmints!" he yelled, surprised to see TWO wombats and furious at the thought of losing the reward money. "Stop, stop! Oi'll get you, you sneaky little animals, if it's the last thing Oi do!"

Beside himself with rage, he flung his cap down on the ground and jumped up and down upon it. When he calmed down a little, he bent down, retrieved his cap and jammed it back on his head. A handful of dust trickled out from under the brim and ran down his face. In a foul mood he stormed along the path to his cottage. When he saw the hole under the door and another in the roof, he realized what must have happened. Muttering darkly to himself, he swore he would catch the wombats and get even with them.

Unaware of the poacher's evil intent, Tambow and Wombi happily trotted beside the gurgling stream, content to be together again, in the late afternoon sun.

They continued at a brisk pace until twilight, when they felt they had put enough distance between themselves and the gloomy little cottage, to feel safe enough to rest. They searched around for a shelter for the night and picked a spot beneath a dense thicket of hawthorn. Nearby, they found a wild cherry tree and ate their fill of the bitter fruit lying on the ground and hanging from the lower branches. Tambow ate rather too many and the noise of his tummy rumbling kept both of them awake for some time.

"Tambow," said his mother, "I'm so proud of you finding a way to rescue me from the poacher. That was very brave of you!"

"I didn't feel brave, in fact I was

frightened without you." Tambow yawned and snuggled closer into Wombi. "Next time perhaps you'll look where you are going!" he said cheekily.

Wombi smiled and listened to his steady breathing turn to a gentle snore as he fell asleep.

6. THE SINISTER WOOD

Dawn came slowly to the sleeping wombats. A dull sky, heavy with storm clouds, gave no encouragement to an early riser. It was only the soft patter of the first rain which woke Tambow and Wombi on their bed of fallen leaves beneath the hawthorn.

Tambow shivered and cuddled closer to his mother's warm body. For a while the hawthorn kept them dry, but soon the rain filtered through the leaves and a large drip landed on Tambow's nose.

Still half asleep, his eyes opened in surprise and he blinked as more rain drops landed on his face. The drips from the tree were becoming steady now and there was no escaping the fact that they were in for a soaking.

Muttering quietly to herself, Wombi struggled up off the leafy bed and poked Tambow with a paw.

"Come on, get up. We're going to get wet whether we like it or not, so we might as well be on our way."

Tambow yawned, wiped the drip off the end of his nose with the back of his paw and asked about breakfast.

"We'll have some more of those berries," said Wombi over her shoulder, as she marched off in the direction of the cherry tree.

After a tummy full of berries washed down by a drink from the stream, the two wombats set off down the valley in the steady rain. Tambow at first tried to step around, or jump over, the rapidly growing puddles, until his paws slipped on the wet mud and he slid into a particularly large puddle. After that, he gave up trying to stay clean and jumped with a great 'splosh' into every puddle he could find.

Wombi looked on disapprovingly, but as even her normally sleek fur was bedraggled with rain and spattered with mud, she held her tongue for once and let him enjoy himself.

Whilst they trotted beside the stream, the normally clear water darkened as the heavy rain lashed the sides of the valley, sending little brown trickles flowing through the heather. The muddy water swelled the stream until it soon became a torrent, washing over the rocks with tumbling waves and licking higher up the mossy banks.

Further down the valley, the open slopes of heather and gorse gave way to a tangled woodland. Once the proud home of some mighty oak and ash trees, but now the best had been felled long ago and carted down to the shipyards on the coast. Around their rotting stumps, alder, hazel, hawthorn and brambles vied with each other for space. Where granite boulders thrust up through the peaty soil, they were smothered by a carpet of moss and ivy.

Into this dark, dripping wood, Wombi led Tambow. The undergrowth was impenetrable, even to a smallish animal like a wombat, forcing them to take a precarious route along the river bank, clambering over slippery

boulders and tree roots.

Mindful of the muddy torrent rushing by beneath them, and of Tambow's accident-prone nature, Wombi insisted he follow closely behind her and stop jumping in puddles.

The rain continued to fall heavily and the stream slowly rose. Underneath the canopy of leaves, the wood was full of noises, rainfall pattering on leaves, the plop of drips landing in pools between the rocks and the growing roar from the stream.

Tambow was picking his way over a tangle of slimy tree roots, a pace behind Wombi, when she suddenly stopped and he barged into her. Ignoring him, she stared back the way they had come, a frown furrowing her furry brow.

"What's the matter, what have you seen?" asked Tambow, following her gaze. He could see nothing out of the ordinary in the grey-green wetness behind them.

"I don't know, I thought... Oh! It doesn't matter, come on," and she turned around again and hurried along the river bank with a new sense of urgency.

Tambow followed precariously, jumping

from one slippery rock to the next and trying hard to keep up with Wombi. The frightening brown torrent, rushing along almost beneath him, put all thoughts of play out of his mind and several times he called out to his mother to slow down, as he was getting left behind.

Each time he caught up, Wombi was looking back through the woods with a worried expression and eventually Tambow asked her for an explanation.

"Well, it's probably my imagination, but I've got a feeling we're being followed by something."

"Oh!" said Tambow. "What kind of a something?" He could suddenly see a lion behind every tree. They had scared him ever since one of the circus lions somehow got into the chimpanzees' tea party. The lion ate all the sandwiches and chased the terrified monkeys up a tent pole before anybody could stop it.

"I really don't know, I expect it's nothing, just this gloomy wood getting on my nerves," and with that she hurried on again, slipping and sliding along the bank.

A little further on, they came to a small

clearing beside the stream. Carpeted with soggy leaves it seemed like a haven amongst the treacherous rocks and thorny undergrowth. A well worn path crossed the clearing and went straight down to the stream, the end of the path already submerged beneath the rising water. Wombi paused at the edge, perched upon a rounded boulder and surveyed the scene in front. Her sixth sense already alerted, although she really did not know why, she wanted to be sure all was safe before crossing the open ground ahead.

She looked this way and that, her nose and whiskers twitching in the damp air, but she could find nothing unusual about the place. Realizing that the path was probably worn by woodland animals coming down to the stream to drink, she decided the clearing must be safe and jumped down from the boulder onto the squelchy leaves. Two short hops and she was able to step down onto the path by the water's edge.

SNAP! Wombi screamed in fright and pain. Tambow, about to jump after her, pulled up short on the boulder in surprise, lost his balance and fell off backwards, landing awkwardly amidst a maze of gnarled tree roots. As Wombi's screams continued to fill the air, he frantically extricated himself and clambered back onto the boulder.

"Wait! Stop, Tambow! Don't come any further," whimpered Wombi when she saw him reappear.

"What's the matter, what's happened?" asked the frightened little wombat. He could see nothing wrong except that she was standing rather awkwardly upon the path.

"My paw's caught ... in a trap." The words came out in a hiss of pain. "Can you see where I jumped down?"

"Yes," gulped Tambow.

"Jump down exactly ...," a grimace of pain silenced her for a moment, "...where I jumped. Step in my paw prints, nowhere else. There may be more traps!"

Tambow did as he was told and came and stood beside his mother. He could see one of her back paws held fast in the jaws of a steel trap. It had been buried in the soft earth and invisible until she unwittingly stepped upon it, her weight releasing the strong spring which clamped the jaws shut. Her initial jump of shock pulled it out of the ground but he could see beneath it a dull steel wire, one end attached to the trap and the other hidden beneath the leaves.

"What can I do, does it hurt?"

"Yes, of course it hurts!" Wombi replied rather shortly. "See if you can prise the jaws apart with your paws."

Tambow gingerly hooked a paw around the contraption and pulled hard. Wombi screamed with pain and Tambow let go of the trap as if he had received an electric shock.

He gently put out a paw to touch his mother's shoulder, and when the pain subsided a little she managed to open her eyes and give him a weak smile.

"I don't think we'll try that again for a little while, we'll have to think of something else." She looked at the trap and realized the flood water was lapping up to it. The stream was rising fast! She took a step up the path, dragging the trap behind her, but was suddenly brought to a stop as the steel wire jerked tight.

She cried in pain again and would have fallen if Tambow had not been there with a steadying paw.

"Tambow, start digging around the wire, I must get this trap free in case the water rises much more." She looked fearfully at the turbulent brown water rushing by, already lapping up to the wire.

Tambow started digging, tearing in with his front paws as he had seen his mother do the previous day. To start with, mud flew out in fine style, but then as the hole filled with water, the mud became slushier until he was digging with his face underwater and coming up for breath every few seconds. Each time he stopped, the mud washed back into the hole and the iron peg securing the wire still held fast.

Thoroughly alarmed now, Wombi gripped the wire with her teeth and pulled frantically, but even when Tambow helped too, they could not get it to move at all. By now, the water level was up to the bedraggled fur on Wombi's tummy and the trap was completely submerged. Try as she might to struggle to higher ground, it was hopeless.

Tambow paced to and fro beside his mother, not knowing what to do. Tears of pain and anguish coursed down his furry cheeks, mingling with the mud and rain. He went and nuzzled Wombi's mud-splashed face and the two miserable animals stood side by side in the rising flood water.

7. A NARROW ESCAPE

Standing on the flooding bank, little Tambow was having trouble staying close beside his mother as the water swirled around his legs. Occasionally small waves, whipped up by the squally wind, buffeted against his flank, threatening to knock him over. Wombi whimpered, the frightened but resigned noise of a small animal knowing that death was inevitable.

Then, over the noise of the rain and the stream, Tambow heard a rustling in the undergrowth and turned around to be almost bowled over by two sleek brown shapes rushing into the clearing. Two otters swerved as they saw the wombats and slid to a halt in the mud.

"Don't hang about here," warned one otter, "the poacher's on his way and he's already caught several woodland folk today!"

"You're not from these parts are you?" inquired the other otter. "You don't look familiar."

"My paw's caught in a trap and I'm stuck. Please help!" wailed Wombi.

Tambow rushed about in the shallows between his mother and the otters, crying, "I tried to dig out the peg, but it's too far under the water. Please help us!"

One otter looked over his shoulder, back into the woods, and then without further ado, he ducked under the swirling brown surface. Tambow anxiously watched and waited as the otter dived under the water. Every now and then his powerful tail would thrash the surface and then disappear from sight again.

Wombi stood quietly, her face screwed up with pain and fear as the water level rose slowly up her flanks. The otter's mate paced back and forth to the edge of the clearing, then shot off back into the tangled undergrowth. A moment later she returned, just as her partner surfaced for a quick breath.

"Hurry!" she hissed urgently, "he'll be here in a minute."

"Nearly done," he grunted, drawing in a great lung full of air, then he ducked out of sight again.

"Tambow, you go on, I'll be all right," Wombi said bravely. "Carry on beside the stream and get as far away from here as you can."

"No, I'll stay here with you," protested Tambow.

"Your mother's right," butted in the otter. "We'll help her, don't you worry. Follow the bank for a little way and you'll come to a small wooden bridge. Cross to the other side and you'll be safe, the poacher never goes there, not since the farmer shot at him once."

Tambow wavered, undecided as to what to do. "Go on!" urged Wombi and the otter.

At that moment, a twig snapped at the edge of the clearing, the branches parted and there stood the poacher. Rain dripped from his battered black hat, past glinting eyes and

soaked into his unkempt beard. The beard parted in an evil grin, to display a gappy row of yellowing teeth as he brought an ancient gun to his shoulder and sighted down the barrel.

Tambow raced off, bounding along the bank like a coiled spring and disappeared from view around a bend. The otter surfaced holding the steel peg aloft in his mouth. His triumphant smile faded when he saw the poacher taking aim at them and he chittered urgently to his mate. They dived from sight and Wombi, frozen with fear, stood alone as the poacher took careful aim and squeezed the trigger.

CLICK! The hammer fell on wet powder and the gun did not go off. The poacher roared with anger and flung the gun down into a bush, then lurched across the clearing towards Wombi, hands outstretched.

She closed her eyes, resigned to her fate, and then suddenly the otters were beside her. "Take a deep breath!" she was told and just had time to do so, when they whisked her off her paws into deep water. As the stream closed over her head, she could hear the enraged shouts from the poacher on the bank.

Her eyes tightly shut and her lungs pounding, the otters guided her along the swiftly flowing stream. One either side, they pressed tightly against her, taking the weight of the trap. Supporting her safely, they brought her up to the surface for a breath.

Time for one quick gasp and down they went again, as they heard a yell from the bank. They carried on downstream, surfacing occasionally to gulp a lung full of damp air, until Wombi thought she must surely drown. Then they surfaced again and the otters looked cautiously around whilst Wombi gasped and spluttered, the pain in her paw temporarily forgotten as she coughed up what seemed like buckets of water.

They passed out of sight of the poacher, who was unable to follow because he stepped on one of his own traps. Hopping around on one foot, he shouted and cursed as he tried to get the trap off the toe of his boot. By the time he freed himself, the animals had long gone. Picking up his gun, he stumped off into the dripping wood, muttering darkly to himself.

Wombi and the otters drifted on down the

stream, buffeted by the swift current. When they were satisfied they were out of danger, the otters gently steered the half drowned wombat to the far bank and helped her out of the water. She lay on the muddy bank until she got her breath back and then she looked down at her back paw, still trapped in the steel jaw. An iron peg trailed from the short wire and a heavy spring kept the trap tightly shut.

The two otters nosed the trap and tried to pull the spring back with their teeth, but it was no use. It wouldn't open and they only succeeded in jerking Wombi's paw, which made her cry out in pain.

"We'll help you down to the bridge to find your son," said one otter, "but then we must get back to our holt. We've left our cubs for too long already."

"Thank you," said Wombi weakly as they lifted her back into the stream and supported her, whilst they drifted on with the current.

Soon they floated round a bend and there in front of them, an old wooden footbridge spanned the stream. As the otters guided Wombi to the bank beneath the bridge, a small shape detached itself from the bushes and Tambow came rushing down to the water's edge.

Jumping up and down with excitement and relief, he cried, "Oh, you're safe, you're safe! I thought the horrible poacher had got you!" And to the otters, "Thank you, thank you for saving my mother, oh, thank you!"

Safely hidden amongst the bushes by the footbridge, Wombi lay on the grass getting her breath back. The otters took a last look at the trap but could not find any way of prising open the jaws. Reluctantly they said they had to leave to return to their cubs, but they hoped Wombi would be able to get her paw free somehow. As far as they knew, the poacher never came down this way so they should be safe from him.

The wombats thanked them for all their help and sadly watched them sliding down the bank, back into the stream. A trail of bubbles swiftly carried away by the current was the only sign of their passing.

By now, the heavy rain had eased to a light drizzle and the grey sky began to be broken up with some puffy white clouds. Wombi's paw was sore and swollen, but not quite so painful. She cautiously tried standing up and found she could limp along slowly, dragging the trap along the ground.

"I won't feel safe until we're well away from this wood, Tambow. I'll try and keep going, do you think you'll be able to carry this peg so it does not drag on the ground?"

Tambow was only too pleased to be given something to do to help and picked up the peg with his teeth, being careful not to jerk the wire joined to the trap.

So the bedraggled wombats slowly made their way out of the wood, Wombi painfully dragging the trap and Tambow walking beside, helping as best he could. As they plodded across a meadow, the rain stopped and the first hint of blue sky was unveiled above them. Half an hour later, their wet fur steamed in the afternoon sun and by the time they reached a little copse beside the stream, they were both dry again.

Once in the copse, Wombi had to lie down to rest. Tambow trotted around looking for a shelter for the night and soon found a cosy spot, if a bit damp, underneath a fallen tree.

He led his mother over to it, and once she was settled down, he went to look for something to eat. Not being used to having to fend for himself, it was all a bit of trial and error. He couldn't find any wild cherry trees, and when he tried some unripe blackberries, they tasted so bitter it almost brought tears to his eyes.

Next he came across some mushrooms and cautiously nibbled at one. Pleasantly surprised, he finished that one off and then pulled up some more, to take back to Wombi. Pleased with his discovery, he came across another type of fungus and bit into it. It was a foul tasting stinkhorn.

He backed away, spitting and coughing, but the smell was so awful that he had to rush down to the stream and put his face underwater. He gargled and spluttered and eventually managed to get the horrid taste out of his mouth. He returned to his little pile of mushrooms and one by one, carried them back to Wombi.

Unconvinced by Tambow's enthusiasm for mushrooms, Wombi suspiciously bit into one, but soon she was helping Tambow reduce the pile with a good appetite. After supper, Tambow asked his mother about her paw and what could they do about the trap.

"My paw hurts dear, but I'll manage as long as I can get this awful trap off. Quite how we do that, I don't know. Perhaps we'll get an answer tomorrow. For now, I'm exhausted and I must try and get some sleep, so should you."

Tambow snuggled close to his mother as the daylight faded in the little copse and was soon fast asleep, but he was to awaken many times during the night as his mother tossed and turned and cried out in pain. Unable to help, he cried himself back to sleep each time.

8. GOOD DOGS AND BAD

The pain in her paw gave Wombi a restless night and soon after dawn, she and Tambow left the shelter of the copse and continued through the field by the stream.

Progress was slow as she dragged the trap from her throbbing paw, but the dewy grass in the meadow had been nibbled short by sheep and was easy to walk over.

At the end of the first field they came to a high earthen bank, topped by a tangled hawthorn hedge. The wombats had a difficult time getting over it as the trap kept catching on the brambles and tugging on Wombi's paw, causing her to cry out. At last she was through the hawthorn and slid down the far side of the bank, into the next field.

Tambow was about to slide down after her, when a rustling in the leaves caught his attention and he pushed a bramble aside with his paw. Beady little eyes peered down a long snout at him and Tambow stared in surprise at the prickly creature.

Before he could even introduce himself, the hedgehog curled up into a tight ball, sharp quills pointing in every direction! Curiously, Tambow put out a paw and tapped the hedgehog, getting pricked in the process. The hedgehog, knocked off balance, rolled over and over, back down into the field, dizzily uncurled itself and staggered off along the hedgerow. Tambow slid down the other side of the bank to join his mother, glad she hadn't seen the heartless action.

At the far side of the field, a flock of sheep grazed quietly, a little distance from the stream. The wombats slowly made their way across the short grass, which was quickly drying now as the sun rose above the trees and burnt off the last of the dew. They followed the fence at the field's edge, separated from the stream by a narrow band of trees, chestnut and beech, alder and silver birch. The roots of the bigger trees grew out into the running water and provided shelter for the little trout that swam there.

Suddenly, there was a commotion among the sheep in front, baas and bleats carried on the wind as the confused animals ran aimlessly into each other. The wombats stopped and looked up to see a huge black hound jump out of the hedge and chase towards the flock. One sheep started running and the rest followed, straight towards the wombats!

Wombi and Tambow pressed themselves down upon the grass beside the fence and cowered as the frightened sheep charged past. Tambow's eyes were as round as saucers as they peeped out from behind his paws. The hound sprinted by, rapidly gaining on the sheep, but then it caught the strange scent of the wombats and intrigued, it slithered to a stop. Some thirty paces beyond them, it cast about with its nose on the ground, then came upon their trail. With a spine-chilling growl it loped towards them, its drooling tongue hanging over great curved teeth.

Tambow was terrified and found himself rooted to the spot. He squeaked feebly when Wombi cuffed him to get his attention and dragged his eyes away from the awesome animal to see what his mother wanted. She had crawled through a small gap in the fence, painfully dragging the trap behind her.

"Come on!" she hissed.

His trance broken, he fled through the fence and would have kept going but then remembered to help his mother. They had barely reached the shadow of the trees when the hound stopped at the spot where they had left the field. It quickly found the gap in the fence and with another growl charged at it. The wombats heard a yelp and more ferocious growls, then saw the fence shaking. The hound had got itself stuck!

Given new hope, Wombi pushed on, ignoring the pain in her paw, and came to the edge of the stream. A little further down she saw a single plank bridge spanning the rushing water and decided to try and make for that. They hobbled on through the trees as the hound pulled itself free of the fence behind them. It cast about for a few moments, looking for another way through, but without success. Undeterred, it trotted a few paces back into the field and then rushed at the fence, clearing it with a great bound. It was straight on the wombats' trail again and came crashing through the trees after them.

As Tambow stepped onto the narrow bridge behind Wombi, carrying the steel peg in his mouth, he heard the awful baying of the hound close behind. Glancing back, he saw it racing towards them and he nearly swallowed the peg in fright. All he could do was follow Wombi across the gnarled plank at what seemed to him like a snail's pace.

As the hound reached the bridge, Wombi was stepping off the other end onto the mossy bank when she stopped with a wail of despair. Two more dogs rushed towards her from the far side. Her spirit broken, she sank to the ground and now Tambow could see them too. Trapped on the bridge, he did the only thing possible and jumped into the swirling water.

Wombi closed her eyes as the two golden brown dogs leapt forward and then felt a rush of wind as one by one they jumped over her and onto the bridge. Looking up in surprise, she saw the black hound pressed back to the far bank by their attack and then it ran off through the trees with the other two snarling and snapping at its heels.

They soon gave up the chase and came trotting back across the bridge to where Wombi lay, amazed at her good fortune.

"You don't look too good," said the first dog. "It's lucky we came along when we did. What's your name?"

"Wombi," said Wombi, "What's yours?"

"I'm Gemma, and this is my sister Abbi. We live over there," she said waving a paw in the direction of a little stone cottage close to the stream.

Seeing that the dogs were friendly, a small soggy figure left his hiding place in a bush and bounded towards Wombi, spraying water everywhere.

"Are you all right Wombi, are you all right?" gasped Tambow, dripping all over her.

"Yes," she smiled, "and you can thank Gemma and Abbi here for that. This is

Tambow, my son."

"I'm a wombat!" said Tambow proudly.

"Oh!" said Gemma, none the wiser. "You can both rest here a while if you like. Who, er, what did you say you were?"

"Wombats," prompted Tambow. "Have you got anything to eat? I haven't had my breakfast yet."

"What do wombats like to eat?" asked Gemma. "I could probably find you a rabbit."

"Oh, no thank you," said Wombi, thinking of Tibbar. "Some berries or roots would be fine, or grass, you've plenty of that."

Wombi struggled up off the ground and the steel trap clanked against a stone. Abbi pressed her nose to it, to see what it was and backed away, snorting. She didn't like it!

When she had blown the smell of the evil metal from her nostrils, she said to Wombi, "You poor thing, how long have you had that trap on your paw?"

"Since yesterday, can you do anything to help get it off?" asked Wombi, plaintively.

But the dogs' paws were too large and clumsy and their teeth could not grip the smooth metal. Gemma sat down and scratched her ear, something she often did when she wanted to think.

"We can't let the master know you are here. He likes us well enough, but he thinks most other animals are pests or his Sunday roast joint. His children are kind. They might be able to get it off."

"Good idea," joined in Abbi. "If we hide them in the stable now, the children will see them this afternoon, when they come to feed the ponies after school."

Gemma and Abbi led the way to the stable, a short distance from the house. The door was ajar and as they approached it, a mouse rushed out, closely followed by a black cat. The mouse ran between Abbi's legs, who stopped in surprise, and the cat crashed into her. The mouse took the opportunity to disappear into a pile of straw.

"Sorry, Sooty," apologised Abbi.

"You hairy great lump, I've been stalking that mouse for ages," she hissed furiously. Then she saw the wombats and she eyed them suspiciously, her back arched. "Who are they?"

"Now don't be unfriendly, Sooty," chided Gemma, "this is Wombi and this is Tambow. They've had some trouble and we're going to help them. They don't eat mice so they won't get in your way. Now, where's Silver? We'd better introduce her as well."

"Someone called?" They all looked up at a sleek grey face peering over from the edge of the roof, whiskers gleaming in the sunshine.

"Come down, Silver, and say hello."

The cat lithely trotted along the roof, her favourite spot for soaking up the sun, and jumped down onto the lid of the water butt and then down to the ground.

By this time Sooty had forgotten all about her lost mouse and bad temper, and the two cats tut-tutted sympathetically over Wombi's paw, before the procession of animals filed into the gloomy interior.

The dusty hay got up Tambow's nose and he felt a great sneeze coming on, as he followed the others across the bed of trampled straw. He shut his eyes as he tried to hold it in and walked into something solid.

"AH, AAAACHOOOOOOSH!" Suddenly,

the something solid hit him in the tummy and he went flying through the air, straight out of the door and landed painfully on his backside.

"Blackie, that wasn't very kind!"

"Hurumph, well I'm sorry," said a deep voice, "but I was having a good dream when that noise woke me up with a jolt. What did I kick by the way?"

"A wombat called Tambow," explained Gemma.

"Oh," said the pony and thought about this for a while as he picked a mouthful of hay from the net in front of him. At length, he manoeuvred the half chewed hay to one side of his mouth and said, in a muffled voice, "What's a wombat?"

"It's an, er, it's well, oh, it's one of these," Gemma finished, drawing the pony's attention to Wombi.

"Oh," said Blackie again, gazing at Wombi with his big eyes. Then at length, "Hullo."

"Hullo," said Wombi, a little nervous at being so close to those large hooves. Tambow returned, cautiously skirting the wall to keep as far away from Blackie as he could, and joined

Wombi.

"And you must be Tambow," said the pony, looking down at him.

"Yes," squeaked Tambow, still out of breath from his sudden exit.

"Honey, wake up," said Blackie, looking into the next stall. A chestnut pony put her head over the wooden partition, blinking sleepy dreams from her eyes. "Have you ever seen one of these before? Wombats they're called!"

"No," Honey yawned, "I don't think I have. What are they doing in our stable?"

"Can you look after them until this afternoon, when the children come?" asked Gemma. "They can sleep in a corner here, don't tread on them, that's all."

Before settling down, Tambow foraged near the stable for something to eat. Wombi had no appetite and stayed in the stable. He found plenty of grass and chewed the succulent bark of some small trees. Gemma knew they were apple trees planted by her master last season, but she didn't want to say anything as he was obviously enjoying his meal so much. Besides, she didn't like apples!

After a drink from Blackie's bucket of water, Tambow curled up beside Wombi in the corner of the stable, comfortable on a dry bed of straw. They wondered what would happen when the children came, and were still wondering when they fell asleep.

9. TROUBLE WITH VEGETABLES

Wombi awoke to hear the laughter and chatter of children outside the stable. A metal pail clanked and the stable door was pulled open, letting the afternoon sun flood in. Motes of dust danced in the sunbeams and Wombi screwed her eyes up against the bright light.

A fair-haired boy walked in, almost hidden behind the armful of hay he was carrying. His sister, dark-haired and a little younger, followed him. She carried two pails, both half full of oats.

Gemma squeezed past them and padded over to the two wombats, who were both wide awake now and nervous lest the children should tell their father about them. They didn't want to end up in the stew pot! Gemma gave Tambow a friendly lick on the end of his nose and then barked softly but persistently.

Jed dropped his load and crossed to the corner of the stable to see what Gemma wanted. The ponies looked on, Abbi stood in the doorway wagging her tail and the two cats sat on a bale of straw, preening their whiskers. All waited to see what the children would do.

"What've you got there, Gemma?" asked the boy, bending down and tickling her softly behind the ear. Then Tambow fidgeted and he noticed the wombats for the first time. "Beth! Come and take a look at these!"

Beth came across, immediately enchanted by the furry animals. "What are they, Jed? I've never seen animals like that before!"

"We're wombats," explained Wombi, for what seemed like the umpteenth time. "We've escaped from a circus but I've hurt my paw, please don't send us back!"

"Oh, you poor thing," cried Beth. "Let me see!"

She bent down and gingerly turned Wombi

on her side and saw the trap. The spring was too strong for her, but with Jed's help they prised it off and tossed it to one side.

What a relief for Wombi, but her paw was still cut and bruised from the metal jaw. Beth fetched some clean water from the stream and dipped her handkerchief into it, then she carefully cleaned the wound.

Meanwhile, Jed rummaged around at the back of the stable and came back with a dusty bottle. "Put some of this iodine on, Beth. Dad used it on Blackie, when he cut himself on some wire."

"This'll hurt a bit," Beth told Wombi, "but it'll make it better."

Wombi hissed with pain as the iodine flowed over her cut paw and Tambow fidgeted anxiously. Then Beth tore a strip off her handkerchief and bandaged the paw neatly.

"Proper little nurse, aren't you," observed Jed. "They'd better stay here for a while until that gets better. They'll be safe from Dad for a few days, he never comes near the stable except on his day off."

"Where are you trying to get to?" Beth asked Wombi.

"Home," she replied, "we live across the sea."

"We went to the sea once last summer," remembered Beth. "We had a lovely time on the beach, Jed fell in a pool and got bitten by a crab!"

"What's a beach?" asked Tambow.

"Masses and masses of lovely golden sand. You can dig holes and make sandcastles and play all sorts of games. There were rocks to climb and the sea to splash in. It was lovely!" Beth sighed, thinking about it.

Tambow thought it sounded lovely too and wanted to go right away. Wombi asked how far it was.

"We went on the train, the railway comes through the village up the hill," explained Jed. "It mostly takes stone from the quarries to the port, but sometimes they'll take passengers. Dad's a quarryman and once on a Sunday they had a special train and all the quarry families went down to the sea for the day. It's not too far."

The wombats had seen trains before, during their travels with the circus. They were a bit like the traction engine, which pulled Tuskany the elephant's wagon. Wombi's ears pricked up at the mention of a port but the children didn't know anything about it. They had stopped at another station, a short walk from the beach.

Wombi stood up to see what her paw felt like. She whimpered with pain when she set it on the ground, but to the children's delight she was able to hop about on three paws now she wasn't burdened by the weight of the trap.

Tambow was so relieved that he went racing around and around in the stable until he nearly collided with Blackie's great head, bent low to retrieve a fallen wisp of hay. With memories of those powerful hooves still fresh in his mind, Tambow quickly scooted away to the safety of a corner.

Footsteps were heard on the path outside and a voice called out, "Jed, Beth, where are you? Come on, it's time for your tea."

"That's Mum! Come on, we mustn't let her look in here." The children rushed to the door and the wombats heard them talking outside. “Just finishing off the ponies, Mum, won’t be a minute.”

“All right, but mind you are no longer.” They heard her footsteps retreating back towards the house.

The children came back into the stable and quickly attended to the ponies, chattering to the wombats as they worked. They learnt their names and heard about Marvello’s circus. Beth wanted to know more about their life in the circus, but Jed dragged her away, lest their mother should come looking for them again.

As they left, Jed said to Wombi, “We’ll come back as soon as we can, but you’ll be safe if you stay in here.”

Gemma grinned and whispered, “See, I told you they would help,” and then she and Abbi bounded off after the children.

Sooty stood up, stretched and turned to Silver, “Come on, let’s go hunting.” The two cats jumped down from the bale of straw and silently crept out of the stable in search of mice.

As the sun settled down for the night

behind the hill, the wombats ventured out into the lengthening shadows to forage for their supper. Wombi's paw throbbed and felt like it was burning, so Tambow ran ahead and returned with some choice offerings. Unbeknown to them, the tasty roots and leaves, which he found growing nearby, were all part of the vegetable patch, lovingly tended by the children's father.

By the time Tambow had gorged himself and Wombi had picked at a few leaves, the neat rows of lettuces, carrots and leeks looked as if an army had trampled over them. Fortunately no one ventured out of the little cottage where lamplight glowed softly at the windows, and soon darkness hid the destruction.

Early the next morning, as the first rays of the sun flooded down into the little valley, lighting up the dew-spangled cobwebs in the stable doorway, the wombats were awakened by Blackie, who prodded gently with his great hoof. Tambow squeaked in alarm and moved behind Wombi.

"Shhh!" whispered Blackie. "The master's

about and he's in a foul temper. You two had better hide under the straw in case he comes in."

They heard a deep voice shouting angrily nearby and without further encouragement they dived beneath the straw. Blackie kicked more over them until they were quite hidden.

Not a moment too soon! The stable door was flung wide open with a crash and the dew fell from the cobwebs in a little shower. A large man stood there, black hair poking out from beneath his cap and a short beard, speckled with grey, framing his face, flushed with anger. Under his arm, he carried a shotgun, and it looked as if he was itching to use it.

Blackie and Honey slowly turned their heads to look at him, their big brown eyes giving away no secrets. Their master looked briefly around the stable and then stormed out, yelling for Jed.

The wombats poked their heads out of the straw, ready to disappear in an instant if need be, and heard Jed answer his father.

"What's the matter, Dad?"

"Come and look at the vegetable patch, some bloomin' animal has been and eaten half of it. Look at my fruit trees, ruined! Have you any idea what it could be? The prints are too large for rabbits!"

Of course, Jed knew straight away who had done it, but he couldn't tell his father. "Perhaps it was a deer," he suggested.

"Don't be daft, since when did a deer leave a mark like that! I've got to go to work now but I'm going to wait up for the little vandal tonight. I'm not having some wretched animal ruining all my hard work, if it's not careful, it'll end up on our dinner table." With that, he stomped off down the path and went into the kitchen. A few minutes later he came out again, having exchanged his shotgun for his lunch sack. He swung it over his shoulder and walked briskly down the garden path, banging the front gate behind him.

Jed watched as he crossed the bridge, heading down the valley road towards the quarry, and as soon as his father was out of sight he ducked into the stable. Both wombats dived for cover beneath the straw.

"It's all right, it's only me. You can come out," said Jed.

Tambow got up and shook himself to get rid of the straw. Wombi had an inkling they had eaten something they shouldn't have.

"You are a pair of duffers!" chided Jed. "Dad's vegetable patch is his pride and joy and now he's furious. I suppose I should have told you to keep clear of it."

"We're awfully sorry," said Wombi, upset to have caused so much trouble, "we didn't realise it was all grown purposely."

"You can tell your Dad it tasted yummy though," butted in Tambow.

"I can't tell him that," said Jed seriously, "or we'd all be in trouble. Don't worry though, Beth and I will tidy it up when we get home from school. It looks much worse than it really is."

Then, noticing Wombi still lying on the ground, he asked, "How's your paw?"

"It hurts more today," Wombi answered, her eyes moist and sad, "it feels so hot and I can't stand on it."

"Oh no, I had hoped you would be all right

to leave today. I'm really worried what Dad will do if he finds you here!"

"Can we just stay here in the stable for another day?" she asked.

"Well, I suppose so. I'll talk with Beth at school today, we'll have to think up a plan. Now that Dad is mad, it won't be safe here when he gets home from work tonight."

"Jed, Jed, where are you? Come on, you'll be late for school."

"That's Mum, I've got to go, Beth couldn't come because it's her turn to help with the dishes."

Tambow followed Jed over to the doorway. Peeping out, he could see the children's mother going back into the cottage after seeing them off to school. He watched the two retreating backs until the children were hidden by a bend in the road. The dogs stood wagging their tails by the gate and now turned away and trotted along the path to the stable.

"Hullo you two, I hear you've got the master mad today," said Gemma, as Abbi sniffed around the ravaged vegetable patch.

"Oh dear, we seem to have caused so much

trouble here," replied Wombi.

"Don't worry about it, some cows got into the garden last month and made a much worse mess than that. Where are you going to go now?" Gemma asked.

"We can't leave yet, my paw is too painful. I don't know what we are going to do," wailed Wombi.

"I heard Jed and Beth talking about you as they left for school. Knowing them, I'm sure they'll come up with an idea," said Abbi, her head tilted to one side as she looked at Wombi, sympathy in her soft brown eyes.

"You must hide in here today," warned Gemma. "The children will be home this afternoon, but until then, stay out of sight!"

"You mean I have to stay here *all* day?" asked Tambow, who wanted to go exploring.

"*All* day," said Gemma, fixing a severe stare on him. "Blackie, make sure he stays here with Wombi, will you?"

"Well," said Blackie, "I'm sure young Tambow and I will find lots of things to chat about, won't we, Tambow?"

"But what about my breakfast?" grumbled

Tambow. “I’m hungry!”

“You can share some of my hay,” offered the pony, “and there’s plenty of water in the bucket. You won’t starve.”

“Er, yes, Blackie,” said Tambow, sniffing the dry looking hay without much enthusiasm. A few nibbles later, he was burying his nose in it, looking for greener hay underneath, when the dry dust got up his nose again and made him sneeze.

“AH, AHH, AAAHCHOOOO!” Tambow exploded, and then he rocketed off to the far end of the stable, frightened that he was about to get kicked out of the door again.

“Don’t worry, Tambow, I won’t kick you again. Now, why don’t you finish your breakfast then settle down to sleep. The children will be home before we know it and hopefully they will have thought up a plan to keep you both out of harm’s way while your mother’s paw heals.” Blackie buried his big nose in the hay alongside Tambow’s, and both started munching together.

10 A HOME TO CALL THEIR OWN

Later that day, the stable door opened with a creak and awoke the wombats. “Where are these animals you’re talking about, then?” said a woman, her long fair hair tied back and wearing an apron over her dress.

Jed and Beth crowded in behind their mother, and pointed out the two sleepy wombats, lying in the straw. “There they are Mum, this is Wombi, who was caught in a trap, I bandaged her paw yesterday,” said Beth.

“Oh, they are cute!” said their mother, “What did you say they are? Wombats?”

“Yes, and the little one is called Tambow.”

“I’m Tambow,” said Tambow, wanting to

make sure there was no doubt as to who he was. “Who are you?”

“Well hullo, Tambow, nice to meet you. I’m Mrs.Trekairy, Jed and Beth’s mother. Now, let me have a look at your mother’s paw.”

Mrs. Trekairy unwrapped the bandage and had a look. “Ooh, that must hurt. Let’s clean it and put on some more of that iodine. It looks like it will heal all right, but it’s going to take a while. One of you fetch some water.”

Whilst Jed went off with a bucket for the water, Beth asked, “Mum, Dad is mad today because of his vegetable patch and I don’t know what he will do if he finds out that it was the wombats that ate them!”

“I expect his temper will have cooled a bit by the time he’s home from work,” said Beth’s mother. “If you and Jed work hard to tidy up the damage, and make sure that the wombats know what they can and can’t eat in future, we’ll try and talk him around to letting them stay.”

Jed returned with the water, then fetched the bottle of iodine as his mother washed and cleaned Wombi's paw. The iodine made Wombi wriggle as it stung, but soon her paw was neatly bandaged again and feeling more comfortable.

Leaving the wombats in the stable, with a reminder to Tambow not to leave, Mrs.Trekairy returned to the kitchen to prepare supper and the children went off to tackle the vegetable patch.

As the sun was getting low over the field beside the stable, the two children replanted the last of the uprooted carrots and finished straightening the rows of lettuces, hiding the gaps left by the wombats. Just in time, they ran back to the kitchen as they heard their father's boots scrunching up the gravel path.

Mr. Trekairy came through the door into the cosy kitchen, to see his family looking at him expectantly. "What's up with you lot?" he asked. "Have I grown two heads or something?"

"No, dear," said his wife, "we were just talking."

"Humphh. Well, I'm just going to check on the vegetable patch to see if any more damage has been done, then I'll be back for supper," he said with a gruff voice.

Two minutes later he was back. "Well, I don't believe it! The patch looks better than it ever has! What happened?"

Beth got up from the kitchen table. "Dad, come with me, there's something I want to show you."

She took his hand and dragged him out of the kitchen door, the others following. Gemma and Abbi joined the parade. Leading him towards the stable, she explained all about the wombats, and finished by saying, "Now they know that they can't eat your vegetables, please will you let them stay? Please?"

Her father didn't answer, but pushed open the stable door and went inside.

"Where are these, what d'you call 'em, wombats? Nothing here but the ponies!" said Mr.Trekairy.

"Tambow, Wombi, where are you?" called Beth. "You can come out now, it's alright!"

There was a rustling in the straw in the corner of Blackie's stall, and two furry heads cautiously peeped out, eying Mr.Trekairy with some alarm.

"Well I'll be!" exclaimed Mr.Trekairy. "Never seen animals like that before!"

Beth and Jed went into the stall and each picked up one of the wombats, bringing them back to their father.

"This one is Wombi," said Jed. "Until her paw has healed she can't look after herself."

"We'll look after them and they won't eat anything from the garden again, Dad," said Beth. "Please can we keep them?"

Tambow piped up, "I'm sorry we ate your vegetables, Sir, but they did taste yummy!"

Jed groaned and looked at his father, expecting him to get mad again. Mr.Trekairy scowled at Tambow, who stared back with big eyes and a soft whiskery nose. Then Mr.Trekairy chuckled and his face creased into a smile. Patting Tambow on the head, he said, "Well mind you don't eat any more. If you behave yourselves, you can stay here if you like."

"Oh, thank you, Dad!" chorused the children with broad grins on their faces. Then, to the wombats, "You can call this home now, come on we'll show you around." Beth put Tambow down, but Jed carried Wombi out of the stable, Tambow and the dogs scampering behind.

In the fading evening light, the little procession walked around the house and the garden. Jed explained that the wombats mustn't eat anything in the garden, but through a wide gate there was a large field with grazing for the ponies, bounded with thick hedgerows.

"You'll find lots to eat in there," he said, "then nobody will get mad at you!"

"I don't think even you, Tambow, could eat enough from there to make the ponies starve!" joked Beth.

"Can I start now?" asked Tambow, who hadn't enjoyed his meal of dry hay very much.

The animals squeezed under the gate and Beth climbed over the top. Jed handed Wombi over to Beth, who put her down nearby, beside a rich patch of grass. Then both children sat on the gate and watched as the two wombats contentedly foraged for their supper.

As the shadows lengthened, a call from the house reminded them that it was time for their own supper. They rounded up the wombats and took them back to the stable.

"It's Saturday tomorrow," said Beth, "so no school for us. We'll see if we can talk Mum and Dad into letting you live in the house with the dogs, but for tonight, stay here again. Blackie and Honey will keep you company."

"Well," said Blackie, after the children had gone. "Welcome to our little family. I hope you didn't eat all the grass in our field, Tambow!"

Tambow was not sure if Blackie was joking or not, but he had a sudden picture of himself as a giant wombat, bigger than Tuskany the elephant, if he managed to eat all the grass. He looked down at his tummy, now feeling very full, but it was the same size as usual.

"No, Blackie, I left you plenty," Tambow replied, as he and Wombi settled back into their bed of straw.

The next day was bright and sunny, and the children arrived at the stable early. They let the ponies out into the field, and the wombats went too. After doing their chores of mucking out the stables and filling the water buckets, the children came back to the field carrying heavy saddles and sugar lumps. Bribed by the sugar lumps, the ponies were soon saddled and the children climbed up. Round and round the field they raced, jumping over fallen logs and whooping with delight. Tambow chased along behind, determined to join in the fun, but with his little short legs he was soon left behind.

Jed cantered back to him, jumped off Honey's back and scooped up Tambow. He sat him on the front of the saddle and then climbed up behind him. "Hold on tight, Tambow!" he cried, and then they were off!

Tambow had to dig his claws tightly into the leather saddle to stop himself being bounced off, as Honey started trotting. Then they were cantering and going even faster. A fallen tree loomed up in front of them and Tambow closed his eyes, sure they were about to crash into it.

"Come on, Honey!" he heard Jed yell, then they were up and soaring over the log, landing with a thud on the far side as he opened his eyes again.

"Wow, that was fun!" squealed Tambow

with delight.

Now, Beth was alongside on Blackie, shouting, "I'll race you, Tambow. First one over every log and back to the gate is the winner!"

"Hold on, Tambow, now we'll go really fast!" said Jed, behind him.

The two ponies raced neck and neck around the field. Each time they jumped a log, Tambow was sure he was going to fall off but his strong claws kept their grip. Over the last log, Honey landed a stride before Blackie, and as they galloped past the gate, she was ahead by a nose.

"Yahoo!" yelled Jed. "We won, Tambow!"

They trotted back to the gate and Beth climbed down. Jed held Tambow to pass him down to Beth, but he was stuck to the saddle. "It's all right, Tambow. You can let go now!"

Reluctantly, Tambow loosened his grip on the saddle, and let himself be passed down. Once back on four paws, he staggered a bit, then trotted over to Wombi, who had been watching from the hedgerow.

"That was fun," he beamed. "Do you want a go?"

"No dear, I had more than enough excitement just watching you," she replied, relieved that he was safely back on the ground.

The ponies were unsaddled and left to graze in the field, then Beth picked up Wombi, and followed by her brother and Tambow, they walked over to the house. They found their mother sitting in the sun outside the kitchen, shelling peas.

"Mum," asked Beth, "do you think we could make a bed for the wombats in the lean-to, with the dogs?"

"I don't see why not," replied Mrs.Trekairy. "There are some old boxes behind the tool shed, see what you can find there."

So that day, the children dragged a big box into the lean-to, which was built onto the end of the cottage. They cut an opening in the front of the box, so Wombi could easily get in and out, then lined it with some straw and an old blanket. Gemma and Abbi watched with interest as their new neighbours were settled in with them.

That evening, after it was dark and the evening was getting cool, Gemma said to the wombats, “Come on, we’ll see if they’ll let us in.”

Although not sure what Gemma meant, Wombi hobbled after the dogs with Tambow at her side. They came to the kitchen door and Abbi scratched at the door and barked softly. “Woof, woof!”

The door opened a crack, light spilling out into the night. Beth peered out and then opened the door wider, letting the dogs into the kitchen. When she saw the wombats following, she giggled, then put her finger to her lips. “Be quiet!” she was signalling.

Tambow and Wombi followed the dogs into the kitchen, and joined them on a rug in front of the warm stove. Beth rejoined her mother and Jed at the kitchen table, an interrupted game of cards in front of them. They, along with the four animals by the stove, looked anxiously at Mr.Trekairy, who was sitting in his armchair in the corner, reading his weekly newspaper. He looked up and raised an eyebrow as the wombats settled themselves on the rug. Then he scowled at the three sitting at the table, but before his face was hidden again behind the newspaper, they saw his scowl change to a grin. Then they all knew, the wombats had found a new home!

Tambow whispered to his mother, "Wombi, I think I like it here. Can we stay forever?"

WHAT IS A WOMBAT?
(for those that have never met one!)

Wombats live in Australia and love to bask in the sun!

They are similar in size to a badger, stocky with short legs.
They have thick fur and a short, stubby tail.
They grow up to about 1 metre (3 feet) long and about 35 kg (75 lbs) in weight.
Wombats kept in captivity make affectionate and amusing pets.

They can be quick in their movements and are able to run swiftly for short distances.

The female wombat gives birth to one young, which is carried at first in her pouch, just like a kangaroo carries her young.

After a while, the young wombat runs free, but stays with its mother for the first year or so.

They like to eat grass and roots, and occasionally fungi and the inner bark of certain trees

'TAMBOW'S WOMBATICAL WANDERINGS'

In this equally appealing sequel to ***Tambow***, ***Tambow's Wombatical Wanderings*** continues to tell the story of how Tambow, a bouncy young wombat, and his mother, Wombi, resume their journey.

Their quest follows a stream down to the coast to find a ship to take them home. But along the way, they have to find out where home is!

On paw, raft, steam train and sailing barge, Tambow blunders through the adventures that unfold in every chapter. His mischievous and inquisitive nature constantly gets them both into trouble, but with endless hilarious moments to lighten the danger of their journey.

Carried along in the adventure, the reader rejoices with them as they discover which country they do come from, and how they will return to it.